COMMUNITI   S
and A
This book shou   re
the last

Little Farmer Joe

04840708

For Toby Berlevy, a boy with nerves of steel – **I.W.**
For Thomas, Jonathan and Mel – **C.B.**

The Publisher would like to thank the charity Farms for City Children for their kind assistance in the development of this book.

They may be contacted at:

*Farms for City Children, Nethercott House,
Iddesleigh, Winkleigh, Devon EX19 8BG*

www.farmsforcitychildren.co.uk

KINGFISHER
An imprint of Kingfisher Publications Plc
New Penderel House, 283-288 High Holborn, London WC1V 7HZ

First published in hardback by Kingfisher 2001
First published in paperback by Kingfisher 2001
This paperback edition published by Kingfisher 2003
10 9 8 7 6 5 4 3 2

Text copyright © Ian Whybrow 2001
Illustrations copyright © Christian Birmingham 2001

The moral right of the author and illustrator has been asserted.
All rights reserved. No part of this publication may be reproduced, stored
in a retrieval system or transmitted by any means electronic, mechanical,
photocopying or otherwise, without the prior permission of the publisher.

A CIP catalogue record for this book is available from the British Library.

ISBN 0 7534 0702 7

Printed in Hong Kong

The illustrations in this book are drawn in chalk pastel.

2TR/0403/WKT/MA/150MA

Little Farmer Joe

IAN WHYBROW & CHRISTIAN BIRMINGHAM

KINGFISHER

It was a long and sleepy ride for Joe.
He woke with the clunk of the car door.
It was dark outside.
He couldn't see the farmyard, but he
could smell animals near.

Aunty Bee came running with a big light.
She said, "Here you are at last!" and she
hugged him.
Uncle Will went, "Hup wee man!"
to show him how bright the country
stars were shining.
He said if they were lucky they
might see bats flying.

Joe said, "I'm not scared of bats."
But he couldn't stop shivering.

Mum and Dad had to get back to the city
to see Gran at the hospital.
Mum said, "Be good and give me a kiss for
Gran to make her better."
Dad said, "Won't be long. See you Sunday –
just two nights."

Joe waved and waved till the red lights of
the car went out.

Aunty Bee carried him up
to his own special room.
Joe asked what was the funny
noise outside?
Aunty Bee said, "That's only
the owls calling tu-whoo."
Then she tucked him up tight.

Joe said, "I'm not scared of owls."
But he wanted the light on as well as the moonlight.

At breakfast Uncle Will said, "Is that dog
bothering you, wee man?"
Joe said, "Will he bite me?"
Uncle Will said, "Och no, Oscar's just a
big old softy. Let's take him with us while
we look around the farm."

First they went to the milking shed
and saw the milk squirting.
Joe said, "I'm not scared of cows."

But he didn't like their horns.

They had to pass the pond and
the geese to get to the horses.
Joe said, "I'm not scared of geese.
I just like running my fastest."

He sat on the fence while Aunty Bee called the horses. Joe said, "I'm not scared of horses."
But he wouldn't hold out apples for them.

He held the bucket so Aunty Bee
could feed the hens and chicks.

Joe said, "I'm not scared
of chickens."
But he didn't like the look
of the cockerel.

They went to see the sow's new piglets.
Joe said, "I'm not scared of pigs."
But he didn't want to get muddy.

They all had lunch with the big men.
One of them showed Joe a mouse.
Joe said, "Do they nibble you?"
And he put his hands deep in his pockets.

Soon it was time to take hay to the sheep.
Uncle Will drove the tractor and Joe rode
in the trailer.
"I'm not scared," he said, but he held
on tight.
When they got to the field, the sheep
came rushing.

And wasn't it a daft sheep that bumped Joe over!
"I'm not scared of you!" he said.
But he jumped back in the trailer, quick.

After supper Joe asked was it time to go home now?
Aunty Bee said not to worry, Mum and Dad would
be back soon.
And how about some hot chocolate before he
went to bed?

It was still night-time when
Joe heard voices.
He could see lights on in
the barn, and Aunty Bee
hurrying across the yard
with her boots on.

Uncle Will saw Joe at the window.
He called out for him to come and help.

The sheep in the barn had her baby inside her.
Uncle Will said, "We've got to help her, Joe.
Can you talk to her? She's frightened."

Joe was scared.
He remembered the daft sheep
who bumped him over.
So he said nothing.

But he reached out to her, and he held her tight.
Sometimes she bleated very loudly, but he held
her steady.
Sometimes she kicked her legs, but he never
let go.
"Don't be scared, sheep," he whispered.
"Don't be scared."

Uncle Will pulled and the sheep pushed
and panted.
All the time Joe stroked her.
And all the time Joe talked to her.

Suddenly there was a little wet lamb
to talk to her too.
Uncle Will said, "Now that was brave!
Well done, Farmer Joe!"

What a big breakfast for Joe
next morning!
Oscar came barging up for
a sausage.
Joe said, "Get down, you
big old softy!"
Uncle Will laughed.
"That's it Joe, you tell him!"

And what a busy morning it was!
First Joe fed the lamb.

Then he milked a cow
and patted a calf.

He fed the chicks and
chased the cockerel.

He booed the geese.

He tickled the piglets.

He rode a horse and told his joke to the big men.

And in the evening he helped put the cows to bed.

Soon after, he heard a car coming . . .

It was Mum and Dad!
They said Gran was much better and
she sent her love.

Oscar jumped up and took Dad by surprise.
"Don't mind him!" said Joe.
"Just say *Get down, you big old softy!*"

Mum said, "Did you miss us?"
Joe said, "I missed you a bit, but come
and see in the barn."

The lamb came running to Joe.
Joe said would Mum like to feed him?
Mum was nervous.
She said she'd never fed a lamb before.

Joe said, "Don't be scared.
Just reach out and talk to him –
he won't hurt you."
And he took her hand and showed her.